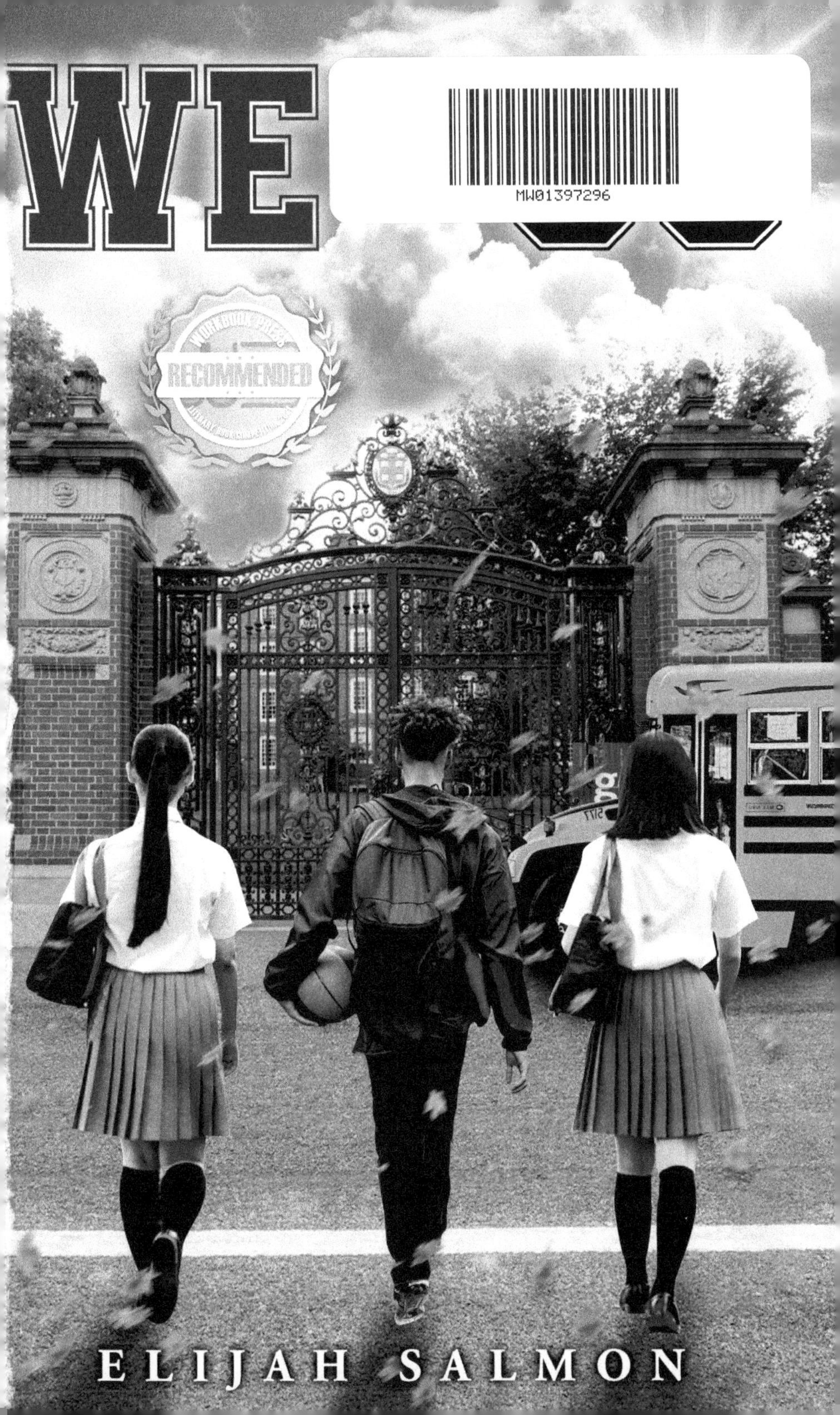
WE
WORKBOOK PRESS
RECOMMENDED
ELIJAH SALMON

Copyright @2021 by Elijah Salmon

All rights reserved. No part of this book may be reproduced in any form or by any electronic or mechanical means, including information storage and retrieval systems, without permission in writing from the publisher, except by reviewers, who may quote brief passages in a review.

This publication contains the opinions and ideas of its author. It is intended to provide helpful and informative material on the subjects addressed in the publication. The author and publisher specifically disclaim all responsibility for any liability, loss or risk, personal or otherwise, which is incurred as a consequence, directly or indirectly, of the use and application of any of the contents of this book.

WORKBOOK PRESS LLC
187 E Warm Springs Rd,
Suite B285, Las Vegas, NV 89119, USA

Website:	https://workbookpress.com/
Hotline:	1-888-818-4856
Email:	admin@workbookpress.com

Ordering Information:
Quantity sales. Special discounts are available on quantity purchases by corporations, associations, and others. For details, contact the publisher at the address above.

ISBN-13:   978-1-956876-40-6 (Paperback Version)
                978-1-956876-41-3 (Digital Version)

REV. DATE: 22.07.2021

WE ARE US

Elijah Salmon

DEDICATION PAGE

This is a way of acknowledging those who have helped me along the way.

My deepest appreciation to....

All those who encouraged me and helped me in prayer, project, and financial support to bring this book to completion; to my mother.

I want to thank also my friends and relatives; this book would not be complete without you.

Most importantly, my gratitude to the Lord and Savior Jesus for His grace and companionship during this project and the Holy Spirit's faithful guidance through this assignment.

THE BEGINNING

There are 3 minutes left on the clock and we are playing in the fall tournament of mixed teams. We are down by 5 points in the 4th quarter and my teammates are exhausted even though she is exhausted and has 4 fouls. She is still determined it looks as if she will collapse. I pat her on her shoulder and say you bring up the ball she nod's and I head down the court. The time is winding down and I look at my team. They look exhausted and depressed. I get into position as she hits half court and she throws up the number 1. I run up and set a screen for her and she runs past me and passes the ball to me at 3 point arch I catch and shoot. The team eyes follow the ball to the hoop as it sinks in the hoop hitting all net.

The team motivation explodes and now the score is 60-62 we are now down by 2 and call a timeout when there's only 1:30 seconds on the clock. As we are going to huddle the team is all hugging me and patting me on the back. We huddle and Lora says good job Pisces and says I know we are up against a solid team and we are a new team but look at how we're doing against one of the well-known teams. If we can just keep it up, we can get to the next round and we hear a whistle blow and we break. The point guard brings the ball up with 50 seconds on the clock. We try not to let the play drag out but that's when they pass the ball to one of their key players. I foul giving me my 5th one. I give the ball to the referee and the team looks at me and I say it's ok we still have me on the court and we have our cap Lora and she smiles. The referee blows his whistle and throws up 2 fingers as he passes the ball.

He bounces the ball twice and shoots, making the first one. We put up our arms to box out and rebound for his next shot. He gets the ball back from the referee and prepares for his next shot. He shoots and misses Lynna rebounds. I run up the court and there's only 25 seconds left. She looks to see me and Lora. I say you can count on me. I can deliver and carry all our hopes, just believe in me, Lora says give it to him! Lynna throws the ball to me as I'm at half court. I catch it and dribble to the 3-point line and shoot as I get fouled. The ball is in the air. It all started when I met two girls trying to start up a mixed basketball team. My name is Pisces Seno. I'm 17 years old and I'm a sophomore in high school. On my way to the orientation, it was being held in the gym, 2 girls were passing out flyers for basketball. I just walk past and one of the girls grabs me by the shoulder and turns me around handing me a flyer and says, "You're short but your body is well-built". I turn away as I move her hand off my shoulder and say, "No thanks. I don't like basketball", and walked on.

I get to a seat and sit with everyone there. They start first with the principal who comes out and says, "Welcome to Spring High", giving his speech. And then have the first group that is recruiting come on stage. I see the girl that grabbed my shoulder, she starts to speak. She says her name is Lananora but she goes by Lana. She is a sophomore and she's 17. She then introduces the other girl saying, "She is my younger sister Anna and we are starting up a mixed basketball team".

I feel as if their names are familiar to me and some other people bring out two basketball hoops and bring out a basketball. She starts to do a simple demonstration and I start thinking that she has skill. Her skills are pretty good too. She calls out a play as soon as her sister finishes them but the speed they are doing this at isn't ordinary. One student speaks out saying what one little imp and gorilla can do alone so what woo you can call out plays and she can do them. It's nothing without talent.

I stand up and say who are you to judge and

walk up to the stage and let's do it again the little sister calls out the plays again and me and the older sister run them. He says What can a pipsqueak do he says you're probably barley 5'5. As he says that I say just watch and see as I think in my head I hope my body can withstand the strain.

    We get started. Anna says we're running different plays being that it's 2 people doing it now I say sure and she asks if I know what the numbers are for mix basketball plays I says yes and she says ok let do 5. I look and say we're starting with that one with a worried look. Lananora says it's ok you throw it to me I say it's fine I can do it throw the ball to me. She looks at me surprised, saying but you, I say it's fine, let's just run it so we can do the next play. We start to go to one of the hoops. Anna say's 5 Lananora throws me the ball. The audience gets surprised to see her throwing the alley-oop one person says there is no way he can get that I jump up to catch the ball with one hand.

    To dunk it everyone goes quiet before Lananora can say anything. I say next and Anna says 3 I passed the ball to Lana and she does a self-alley oop and then 7 gets called I get passed the ball and shoot it hitting all net. I started feeling my sickness acting up. The 2 sisters notice something off and call the last play so I can give it to Lana. She says 1 I throw a quick pass to her and she does a fading 3 pointer shot. I say that you all know about a thing called A.R.T that makes people with them have unique skills in sports that make them better than the average person and these two have it.

You all know that you need a certificate to be allowed to start a mixed team and to qualify to be a player and coach. I leave the stage and head towards the exit after I grab my bag. After I leave the gym I head straight to the bathroom and my body starts hurting from my illness. I take my medicine and head out of the bathroom. When I walk out I see the 2 sisters, I say can I help you Lananora and Anna? They look at each other and I say well if there is nothing I can do for you I'll take my leave. Lananora says you played before, haven't you someone as talented as why do you hate basketball. I put my head down and walk away as I am. She says come play with us and be a part of our team. I look back and say I will not ever return to the court again and walk away. I say in my head it's not that I hate it. It's just because of what happened to me in middle school that has made me scared to return. Since then Lananora has been persistent for 3 weeks straight.

On my way out of the school after putting on my shoes at my shoes locker. She turns and says I know why you stopped playing and that you don't hate the game after all where the 2 that brought you to the game. I look up to see both of them smiling and to see their hair is different. When I look at them I start to say what you mean I get a good look at them I start to see my 2 childhood friends. I call Lananora, Lora and Anna, Anne by accident because when I was 8 I knew 2 girls, one had her mother blue eyes and red hair and the other had hazel eyes with blonde hair. Lananora says you finally remember us, Yin. I say no no way you can't be them they left me back when we just turned 9 you can't be them. I say I just had a lapse in identities. Anna says look at us look past how we look now and look at us yang I shout don't call me that you're not them.

Anna and her sister take out their contacts to show me their real eye colors. Anna says, "Look... look it's us yang, I say again don't call me that you are not Anne". Lananora says, Yin in a sad voice as she tries to walk towards me with her arm clinched on her chest. Saying Yin you really can't recognize us, that's not true right, you could always find us or identify us no matter how we disguise ourselves when we were little. There's no way you couldn't identify us now right. Not just because our hair is different right, our eyes are still the same, just look at us. She says please please Yin look at us I look at them again I look in their eyes. I look at them. I first look at Lananora when I look into

WE ARE US

her red eyes, I start to see Lora. She says, "Do you recognize me? It's me, Lora, it's me Yin". Then I looked at Anna, her hazel eyes started to remind of Anne. She says "Yang Yang, do you recognize us Yang?". I just put my head down and ran past them. I ran out of school to the gate as it started raining. Just as I reach the main gate I find myself falling. When I open my eyes I see Lananora on top of me hold herself up with her eyes open. She says Yin Yin it's us and starts crying Yin Yin we finally were reunited. Please please say you

recognize us. He puts his hand on her face, looks into her eyes and says "You both really did dye both of your hairs". I'm sorry for not being willing to admit it until now. She says you can tell it us know I say the rain is washing you dye away. Lora looks at some of her hair she grabs and says thanks to it getting washed away you can finally recognize us. We get up. I say I already did but I was still in doubt until I saw the true color of you guys hair and if it was really you 2 I would be ashamed to face you 2. I ask how the 2 of you found out it was me. I Didn't tell you my name. Lora says we found a classmate from middle school and they told us what happened to you in middle school, Anna says we didn't really find him. He came up to us after he saw us trying to recruit you. He said you mind as well give up on Pisces. That's when

Lora grabbed him and said his name is Pisces he said yes he stopped after he had collapsed on the court and no one knew why he did. So we guessed the reason was because of his illness. I put my head down and say I can't return. I can't have that happen again. As the rain gets heavier Lora hugs me saying come back please we need you I say as I push her off saying I can't not ever again. Anne says Yang we missed playing with you didn't it feel great running those plays with us 3 weeks ago didn't we do just fine? I say that's different. Anne asks how is it different, doesn't it feel just like when we were little when we dragged you into it. Lora says we know you continue playing after we left so you could find us. We know even with the height difference of the other players you became one of the top players in middle school even with your illness. We…we also know you collapse during a major tournament. I say don't bring that up. Lora said that it isn't because of that. I say what can I do with a frail body like this, how far can I really make it, how long will I be able to be by you two sides before you guys go off and leave me again. I can't take if I'm left behind by you 2 because I can't keep up. Besides, it's been 2-3 years since I last played, you saw how I was during that last play. Anne tries to walk up to me and I turn away and leave. It's been 2 months' sense then and now it's march 16. Tomorrow is my birthday. Lora and Anne have succeeded in making a mixed basketball team and I haven't spoken to them since. Though I catch a glimpse of Lora looking at me with a sad expression on her face. When I was putting on my indoor shoes, Anne came up to me and gave me a ticket to their first game against Soda high. My facial expression went dark and I shouted Why are you 2 doing this why them. As everyone at their shoes locker looks over to us. I bang on my locker. I said I'm not going to go take this back. Lora comes over and says we knew you would react like this but we want you to keep it. We know you are still scared by what happened but please come watch us play. You won't miss a major event for us right Yin. Anne says you always have been our support. You didn't forget our reason and promise for why we went through all that training and then dragged you into it right and smiled at me as the bell rang. I fall to my knees and Anna says it tomorrow. We hope that we can celebrate your birthday with you and that you can understand the first present we are giving you and hope we can give our second one. Then she leaves and I get up and go to class. By the time I was back to myself it was the end of the day and the weekend started tomorrow also so was their first game and my birthday. Before the game started Lora asks Anne if she saw Pisces she shakes her head no. Lynna comes up to them and says the game is about to start. I know my big brother will come. Anne says but does he know about you being here too she shakes her head. After that incident my brother left home and hasn't come back. He sends letters sometimes just to let mom and me know he's ok. The Referee says time to get in position and they head out onto the court. Meanwhile as I am at home working out lifting on dumb bell in one hand and doing my home work with my other. I take a break and lay on my bed as soon as I do I hear banging on my door. And shouting, "Pisces Pisces what are you doing? Are you really not going? Are you just going to abandon them? I get up and head to the door and speak as it's closed saying Luna why are you here aren't you supposed to be at the game you're a player right. She says fine just forget the promise and reason of why they are trying so hard in this league. I open the door and say you have no right to bring that up after how you abandoned us all first with an enraged expression. She says at least I'm trying to move forward and leaves saying what about you. I shut the door and slide down sitting. I say at the end I'm going to go anyway. I put on my shoes and grab my jacket and head to the school. At the game it has 2 minutes left in the 3 quarter. The score is 30-35. Anne says Lynna we need you to play the post more, use your slim build and agility to get by your defender. Put your hands up more don't be scared to make contact. Alexis you're doing fine but try to utilize the plays more. Lora we need you to focus, you're off your game, you're better than this and we can do this. She says I know I know but and the buzzer goes off and they head back on to the court but Lora looks in the crowd again to see if Pisces is there. Then focus back on the game. When I get to the game it's the 4th quarter with six minutes on the clock and the score is 40-44. I see my little sister with the ball and she's double teamed. I think what she is doing here, she passes the ball to Lora. She shoots it from three and it goes in as she runs down the court and sees me, Lynna jags up to her and asks what she's looking at. She points towards me. Lynna and Anne look to see what she is pointing at. They realize that I have come to see them play and smile at me. I head to a spot behind the team Anne walks up to me and says you came with teary eyes. I said don't get the wrong idea I'm not coming back ok she smiled and said well see about that. As I'm about to say what do you mean by that she walks away. Anne claps and says now let's pick it up and I feel then the determination from them it's as if I can hear it. Trying to call me back to the court I hear from Lynna big brother this is where you belong you're the reason I can stand on the court. Anne says I know it was difficult for you but that day it felt as we became one me, you and my sister didn't you feel it don't stay in the dark don't hide anymore come back. Lora steals the ball back and fly by the bench it all went white like all I could see is a white area and her jersey hearing her say Yin you didn't forget right you still remember the promise we made and the reason me and Anne still play right and the white area disappears and she dunks it after she does all 3 of them look at me as if there saying come back I can feel the intent from their eyes. As I'm getting up to leave I hear my little sister scream. I look back to see her on the ground in pain holding her ankle. I run on to the court and hold her in my arms saying are you ok Lynna. She looks up to me and says Yin yin it hurts me to see you like this. I know you still love the game of basketball. The way you looked the last few years you been trying to tear it out of your life it has looked as if you have become life less that not my big brother the brother I know is the one that looks the coolest when he flying up and down the court or when you do a faint into a shot but the best moment is when you're flying through the sky and dunking it. Please don't say you hate it anymore it tears all of our hearts apart mine, mom, dad, Anna, Lana's even Luna's. I say shh we need to get you to the hospital she says I am not leaving this court until I see you come back and be where you belong I say Lynna and the other look at me. I say fine, have it your way and help her up then I return to my seat. Lynna says I'm ok and they resume. Lynna limps to position and the ref blows his whistle and throws 2 figures up and gives the ball to the player at the free throw line. They miss the first one and make the next one. Lynna inbounds the ball to Alexis and she brings the ball up to half court and throws up one. Lynna barely makes it up in time and sets the screen and heads to the post after Lora gets the ball. I see Lynna getting pushed around and banged under the rim. I closed my eyes. She chose this, this was her choice. Lynna tries to get the rebound but her ankle throbs as she tries to jump and miss the rebound. Soda high school gets the rebound and they run down the court. As my eyes are still closed I hear a thud and open my eyes to see Lynna on the ground. I get up Anne says are you really going to let us fight alone for the dream the promise that we made alone? Are you really going to let her stay on the court in that much pain? I say she chose this, it's her path to travel Anne says is that, how you really feel. I shout what do you want me to do of course I don't want the 4 of you fighting alone of course I don't want my sister in pain. What can I do? She chose this and even if I wanted her to sit and take her place we don't play the same position and I'm not a member of the team. By the time I realized what I said all 4 of them were around me smiling at me. I stumble back and I look to see what Lora is holding. I see a jersey with my old number on it, the number I used since we were kids. The number 20. Luna says I knew you didn't forget and wouldn't abandon the promise we made as a group and the reason Anne and Lora are playing, I see a piece of paper saying member Pisces and I put my hand on the jersey and say you guys planned this didn't you they smile and say happy birthday. I put on the jersey and say where in luck the players from back in middle school aren't playing today so we can get by with me playing at 45% but don't think I'll be able to play like I used to. It will take a while. Lora says just rely on your teammates. Anne switches the lineup putting me at the pointe Alexis as shooting guard, Luna small forward, Lora power forward and Lynna center. I say we have 3 minutes left, let's show them what we can do and head on to the court. Lora inbounds the ball to me. I start to dribble up Lora goes up and gets into position and looks at me. You can feel the shift in our team with me on the court and you can tell that their confidence has improved. I just smile and throw up 7. Lynna set the screen. I passed the ball to

Lora and I cut to the basket just by the Shrek from my shoes Lora threw the ball to me. The next thing you see is me in midair. I catch the ball with one hand dunking it. The other team and audience go into shock from the play. The team just looked at me as they smiled as if they knew I had returned. I say no slacking, get back on defense, let's keep the pressure up. Anna says defense set 6. The other team snaps out of it inbounding the ball I get in my defensive stance. The point dribbles a little and I hold my ground and he passes it and runs to the next spot. With the score being 44-45 you can feel the tension from both teams causing them to fumble a pass and Luna gets it passing it to me. I run up the court shooting a three and as it sinks in making the score 47-45. Then the crowd erupts into cheers. I say know Anne, we're going to rely on you to run the show now. She says got it and calls play 3 to slow down their offence. I get in position and wait for their point guard to come up. I start to feel the effect from me not playing for 2 years catching up to me. I wipe the sweat off my four head. The point guard reaches me and tries to post me up as he turns away. I hit a well-built player landing on my back. I hear a whistle blow and I hear Lora yell my name as she's running to me. I sit up and say I'm fine, it's nothing. She helped me up and the ref said the offence of foul on 25. Springs High's ball with 1:08 seconds on the clock we're in the ideal situation for our first game especially for going against one of the mixed teams that one spot from being called a giant. Then again their key players aren't here so we need to take this chance. I get the ball and head up the court. I really start to feel the exhausting catching up to me. I put up 4 and ran to Alexis, passing the ball to her and setting the screen and going to the corner three. Alexis dribbles trying to make her way to the paint and gives up passing the ball to Lynna in the post. She tries for a hook shot as it clings off the rim. Lora goes in for the rebound and gets it but fumbles it. Soda high gets it with 20 seconds on the clock they rush up the court and pass it to the wing player at the half court he runs to the three-point line greeted by Luna. She is in the top 15 of the fastest players in the mixed league. It is not easy to beat her on the court. He stopped from shooting it and passed it to the shooting guard and I greeted him. With 5 seconds on the clock he shoots it. I jump and just barely nipping the ball enough to change the shot but it still heads to the hoop. It hits the rim and rolls around with the time at zero we all get nervous. The ball stops for a moment. It feels as if we stopped breathing just then the ball starts falling off we all start cheering and the ball hits the floor and the buzzer rings we break out into cheering and hugging each other. I get lifted up and tossed in the air but as I am someone comes up to us and says so you finally came back if I had known I would have played. I think that voice can't be. I say Zack so you were here he says it seems you didn't fully recover from 2 years ago or is it that you don't plan on sticking around and abandoning your teammates again. I bit my lip and looked away. Lora steps in and says what are you talking about he would never do that. He laughs and says so he didn't tell you did he. Anne says we know about the game and why he stopped. Zack says but did he really explain what caused it I say Zack he says oop oops well I just came to say hello and leaves. The team gathers around me. I say, "Let's talk in the locker room". We get there, Luna says what he was talking about Pisces Lora, Anne and Lyna says, explain what he meant. I say after they found out about my Illness they still wanted me to come back and continue to play with them I... I Lora says out with it already. I say they had been told about my illness after I had already quite the team. Someone had told them Lyna says what did you say to make him say that about you. I... I told them that I had let my illness build up to then and that I was tired of playing basketball and that I wanted out. They all looked at me with anger but Anna had tears in her eyes.

Alexis says so what about you not staying with or that you're not recovered from then. I say I… I'm sorry I could have played a little better but not much. I just wanted my sister to get her ankle looked at so I lied about how well I could play. I only played to make sure we had a chance to win. I get smacked by all 4 of them and Lora asks, ``Are you going to leave us know when I am about to answer? I see that the teams have tears in their eyes. I say no I'm not with all my might and say I was going to but after I saw how much you guys fought to get it through to me to come back how can I not come back and smile. I get a group hug and Lora says welcome back home Pisces and I'm glad you didn't forget our promise and reason yang yang. Lyna says don't ever leave us again big brother yin yin. I say I'm not going anywhere. They let me go. I say now we may have made it to the next round but being that Zack knows I'm back our games won't be easy the next time we play them in semi-finals all 4 of their top players will hit us with everything they have and so will the other teams. The biggest concern I'm worried about is the 5 kings coming to watch. Luna says you're right, especially being that we have 2 of them on our team. I say I can no longer be called one of the kings with the shape I'm in plus it would be 3 if Anne were to play. I ask how that injury that you had got last year. She looks at me like how did I know I say I'll tell you in a minute but the kings also have 2 of our childhood friends even though she isn't a player but a coach she is still a force to be reckoned with. Luna says the twin Selene and Aurora. Lora says well hit that bridge when we get to it know Pisces how did you know about Anna. I say I might have stayed away from basketball but I would hear about you two once in a while, never heard the school you went to but I still heard info about you too. You to Lynna you went to school with them she says how did you find out. I say I'm your big brother of course I keep tabs on you. One of my friends told me that you had lied about the school you went to. She walked up to me and tugs on my jersey. I pluck her on her forehead and say let's rest and get ready for the next game.

As I'm walking away I feel my illness start to act up. A sharp pain shot up my legs causing me to lean on the locker. Luna catches me, Lora and Anne run up to me and help me sit. Lyna asks me if I'm ok. Is it my illness acting up? I say I'm fine Lora says you're not playing the first quarter I say but we're going against stone high I have to play. Anne says where's your medicine? I say don't give it to me, give me the ibuprofen or otherwise if you give me my other meds I won't be able to play and she says ok but you need to rest. I say you guys wanted me to come and know you want me to sit out of the next game. This is why I didn't want to come back but you guys wouldn't listen. I'm playing in the next game. Lora says Yin relax were not sitting you out the whole game. Rely on us more remember you have us know and don't forget me and Anne are also queen players and we have 2 giants on our team Luna and Lyna. Plus, Alexis has the defensive arts that makes her a candidate for being a giant so you can at least rest for a quarter or 2 as we play. That should give time for the ibuprofen to help relieve it.

I say fine I'll sit for the 1 first quart maybe the 2 second one depending how things are. Lora and Anne smile at me and say that's our future husband without thinking. I say hey with an embarrassed look on my face. Alexis says ahh so that the promise you guys made they blush as Luna puts her hand on her face. I say anyways it is only a few minutes until our next game let's warm up so our bodies don't go cold. Anne says wait we didn't tell him one more thing Lora says oh yea she turns around and says what the lineup is and says captain welcome back to the game I say w..what me the captain I thought Lora was. She says did you ever hear anyone call me that or anyone else captain I say you sneaky little and they all run past me out of the locker room as I chase after them. We get to the gym and walk in when the stone high team stands in front of our bench we walk up. One of their players says that you really came back after 2 years of being a ghost and claps so I'm guessing these 4 brought you back. I say Max, you look well what happened to you being a bench player at Omaha high with king Isaac. He says oh that well I transfer so I could put those snootie twins in their place. I say you can barely handle a giant what makes you think you can do anything against them. He says that was middle school my ranking changed I'm a rank 16 giant know I look to Luna and think that only one spot behind her and with his arts of eagle eye and lock on which pin point out which player or plays a team run for a shorten amount of time Luna and Alexis will be in trouble even with her speed and Alexis evasion. He says that right you can't rely on those too depending on your plays. I look at him and think I'm in no condition to play the first full 32 minutes. Just when I'm about to open my mouth Anne puts her hand on my shoulder and says well then I might just have to hit the court with my sister he steps back. Lora and Lyna step in and say you haven't forgotten about us right. He says but Anna you still injured aren't you the impeccable ice queen and aren't you limited without the 2 nature god Pisces. Goddess of fire Lora, Lora says don't forget princess of wind Lynna he says but isn't she at the school of ruler with her older sister goddess of wind I say come now don't you see my little sister right here as he looks to my left. He says the 4 of 11 gods/goddesses are here. I say Lyna isn't a goddess yet so 3 and just because of your arts doesn't completely mean Luna and Alexis are out, don't forget one is the princess of night and the other belongs to the lighting elements. He clicks his tongue and walks away. Lora says no matter what you do, do not come in for the first quarter. Anne, you think you manage 1 or 2 quarters as Luna sits on the bench with Yin. She says yea I should be able to handle it but idk about any longer than that. I say no, you only play 1 quarter, maybe half of the 2 second depending on how things go. She says you worry too much. I say well for our line up to be complete we need you to be healthy for the other rounds and tournaments. She smiles at me and gives me a kiss on the cheek and says I will be fine as I stumble back and say not in front of everyone and Lora says aww I wanna kiss him too. I say let's go blushing. The whole team laughs and follows me so the starting lineup is Anne at point, Alexis at 2, Lora at 3, Lyna at 4, and Jin at 5. They head on to the court to get ready for the jump ball. I see Stone high starting lineup to see Max on the bench. When I look back to the starting lineup I see number 21 I get up and Anne says no. I say but that's when Lora says we know I say then why you know that she's a queen candidate with Anne hurt the only one we have to stand against her is you Lora and the rest of their team aren't pushovers. Even with Lyna and Alexis on the court things could go very bad in the first half. Alexis says have some faith in us. Remember when we were in middle school who used to be the 6 ruling players I say true but Lora cut in saying you may be the 2 element god but me and Anne are the ice and fire goddess with the princess of wind. Princess of night Alexis says remember I'm the night princess for a reason and I will be taking the title goddess of moon from sister making her the princess. I laugh and say you guys are right but remember she has the capability of changing my big sister for the god of wind so don't let her fly. They respond saying leave this to us. She notices me and walks towards me. I get up and meet her. She says I saw the last game I was hoping to play against you that's why I had Max sit. After 2 years of just leaving the game you finally come back. You, one of top 3 Ruler the god of 2 elements Pisces along with the goddess of earth Lexis the great god ice Leon. Only if them and the other 5 rulers were here the Goddess of moon Jane, the sun god Manny, goddess of lighting Mercedes, the twin goddess of nature

Selene and Aurora. that's when they pop up all of sudden. Mercedes says when we heard about Pisces we just had to come see if all the pictures and messages were true and it was actually true it's actually you in the flesh. You came back after 2 years; you're not sitting on the bench after only playing one quarter right. You are going to start after all we all came to see you in action again. That's when the 2 of the 3 top rulers come out and say of course he is playing right and Leon comes in behind Lexis. I walk up to them Leon says so the 3 rulers back in the same gym again. Lora, Anne walk up behind me and say Leon, Lexis. Anne says of course he is playing but being this is first time playing competitively we wanted him to sit for 1-2 quarters. Lexis says the one that made the deadlock between us is tired after only one quarter that can't be right. I say of course not. I can play the first 2 quarters just like we used to when we 3 where duded as the top 3 players in the country. Leon says, looking forward to seeing you fly again. One of the people in the crowd sees us and says oh my god the 10 rulers are all in the gym. Then you hear what it can't be Pisces came back, wait Lexis is here too. Jane says we should sit before things get out of control and stop the game. Leon says right and they sit behind the team's bench. Lora asks me if I can handle playing 2 quarter or more I say I have to because all the ruler is here with me being in the top 3 I have to put on the display I'm still in top shape but listen Anne, Lora I'm going to need you stay on the court as long as I am on. I know it might put a lot of strain on your injured shooting arm. She says as long as you need us we will be there. I smile and say let's go. The referee says it's a lineup change for spring high; the lineup is now Pisces, Anna, Luna, Lora and Lynna. The crowd breaks out saying he finally came back; we knew you would come back. Welcome back Pisces the game wasn't the same without you. Boo boo how dare you come back after leaving your loyal fans and teammates. Anne covers my ears and says tune them out. Focus on the 4 of us. I look to see the other 3 looking at me with worried eyes. I say I'm fine, let's do this. The ref blows his whistle and throws the ball up and Lyna jumps, tipping it back to me. I get it and start dribbling. I get that look from Anne saying show that you're back playing at top shape play like you always do well back you I smile and nod. I let the ball bounce the throw up 20. Lora says finally you going to play like the player you are I laugh Lora set a screen I blow by and a Cleo come to me I dribble when I do it has smooth as water but furious like a river and when I go by it has if a gust of wind is pounding you and I go by I fake a dunk a go to a fade away. As I am doing my fade away, my motion is like water flowing and when I release it's as if it is being guided by the wind hitting all net. We get back to defend and Anne takes over. She calls out 3 and we get into position. Cleo comes up. I say you're not the candidate for nothing for the goddess of wind but do you really think that enough to get past me. She says let's find out it turns into a one on one between me and Cleo. She dribbles between her legs and tries to cross over. I cut her off then she goes for a half spin. I shift a little. she tries the post to back me down a little and cross between her legs again. He shoots, my jump is delayed and she makes it. She says let's go all out I say you sure you can handle me she says you're not in top shape your shell of your former self I say you might regret saying that. Lyna inbounds the ball to me. I dribble up, I call 5 and give the ball to Anne. She gets a screen from Lora and fakes a shot and throws me an alley-oop. I catch it with one hand and slam it in on their center. Lexis says for him to be gone for 2 years and still be able to be in shape to pull that off. Leon says he only warming up that wasn't even 50% of true potential and he was still able beat Cleo and she play at 55% and with the way he playing it only to fuel Lora and then it gonna get Anna going and once the other 2 get going even with Max ability there going to have a hard time dealing with them unless. Lexis says unless Pisces exhausting catches him first plus Lynna and Anna are hurt so if they play on that the game might go differently. Lexis says but the outcome of the game isn't what the 7 of us are here for. It's to see if Pisces is still at the top of his game or if he has fallen from the reins of being called the 2 element god and being in the top 3 so within the 64 minutes it will determine how he and the rest of the league shapes up going forward. Anne inbounds the ball to me. I come down the court and I'm a few feet from the 3-point line and pull up the rest of the team head back once I release it I head back to. Cleo says I see you as confident as always but then again when hasn't a shot you put up hasn't hit the bottom of net as he says that it hit the bottom of net making the score 5-2. I say you know who you are dealing with, you better kick up those gears before the 4 get going and bring in max or it's going to be a long game for you. She says you right I have always been unable to match even when I'm at 50% it takes less for you to match it. So let's show you why I'm one of the candidates and get this game on the right track when a gust of wind from us collides. Jane says now we are about to see the true battle between king and candidate. I say Lora, Anne and the others get ready let's show them our power you guys handle the other I got Cleo. Anne says but you I say don't worry I'll last until the end of the game. Anne says there is no way... As she fell Lora hand touched her shoulder and looked at her and knew there was no way to avoid this. Anne says you all heard cap let's not let him down and the rest of the team says right. As Cleo stands in front Pisces as the wind from them starts colluding against each other as if blows were being thrown at each other in a boxing ring. Cleo is crossing over and trying to spin by Pisces but she is getting shut down Cleo goes for hesitation but that also doesn't work then she decides to go for a fade again. Pisces reacts a little too slowly but manages to contest the shot the ball hits the rim and bounces in. The game tempo changes and Lyna runs and get the ball inbounding it to Pisces I dribble up and again it as if they are throwing blows in a boxing ring I cross over she doesn't go for it I post her up and spin doing a fake step back and pass to Lyna she does a post hook shot and makes it making the score 7-4. We hear a whistle blow stone high call time out for a sub and Max comes on the court and number 5 gets sent out. I say you 4 it time for you to shine. You guys warmed up right? I can take a break right. Lora says count on us, take a break, just focus on passing and defense leave the scoring to us. I say ok after our next offence play it will be on you guys. Cleo brings up the ball and it's a clash between king and candidate Cleo dribble and cross over trying to go for a blow by, but Pisces pokes the ball making her fumble it and she gets it back. She throws up 3 and Anne says 2 and we switch. I go to max and Anne goes to Cleo. Everybody gets surprised by the switch. It's the ice queen versus the candidate for the goddess of wind. Who will come out on top. Cleo says are you sure you can keep up with me with your injury ahh wait then again it is your arm that injured I forgot. Anne says you sure you wanna sit there and talk as Lora comes up and steals it from behind. I take off down court and Lora passes it to me as I'm at the free throw line and I catch it and go right to dunking it. Anne says you should be focusing on yourself. I get back to the others and says know let's switch up our game play and after 2 minutes I will sit until the time hits 8 minutes. Leon says this is not going to go well for them without him. Lexis says it won't because we are part of the top 3 rulers that this is an act only the 10 rulers know that Max is part of the lost time element family. There's only a couple of them in the pro mix team league they can make it look as if time has skipped or stops. Once they catch on to Pisces is recovering on the court and then sitting half way through the 2 quarter they will take advantage and only with

Lora and Anne plus she injured they won't last long. He may have to play like he was back to normal but he's only at 79-82% but you can say he's back because if things hold at how they are because he made sure to let Lora, Anne, Lyna warm up and be in a favorable position. He will be able to hit that 85% and don't even minchin the spring tournament. We will see him back to his normal self. But right now if he has to activate the 3 god element that the top 10 rulers know about he will be seriously hurt. Leon says everyone thinks it was his illness that kept him away from the game but it was he activated the 3 elements before he was ready which caused his illness. Lexis says if he only uses his water he would be at 85-90% and they are taking advantage of that. We can say though the one that holds the deadlock between us is back. Lexis says isn't that why we let him hold the number 1 spot among us because the 3 of our potential were in a deadlock. Being that we hold arts our body develops faster so we will be fully developed after we started high school. Leon says there putting their plan in motion Pisces brings up the ball he says 10. As a screen is set for Lora then Anne I pass the ball to her and run to the side. Cleo says wait Anne got the ball and realizes the plan but it's a little too late and she alley-oops the ball to her sister she catches it and slams it with both hands pushing the defender out of the way and she comes down. She realizes the 2 other rulers have awakened by how the ball touched their hands. This doesn't bode well for us and thinks and says wait why didn't Pisces get involved. It clicks but she decides to test it first. She gets the ball and brings it up Anne meets her she says you plan on resting him don't you Anne reacts. She says I knew it but are you sure you can before she gets the chance to finish I try to steal it. She says ahh come on now we were having a nice chat. Anne says go back. I say Anne focuses and she snaps out of it and says no worry I got this but Cleo takes advantage and passes to the open man for a 3 and makes it. Making the score 9-7 with 9 minutes on the clock. She says before she goes back down court don't forget why they call me the queen of ice, she laughs and says show us that power and goes down court. I inbound it and went up. She says 8 we all go back to defense and she goes in between the half court and three.

 The other team looks confused and Cleo says no it can be your shooting arms is injured before she shots she says that was on purpose so you would be dumb enough to let your guard down and you should know not to tease a top 10 ruler power when she releases it the air seem as if it's starting to become chilly and the ball is beginning to look like an ice cube. The shot sinks into the bottom of the net as she runs back down court a Cleo toss and says inbound the ball to me and I'll take on Pisces. Just as she's dribbling the ball up the court the door bursts open and three people come through it and one of the girl's shouts Pisces is that you, you are really playing again. Cleo stops dribbling and we look up to where the voice came from. I look to see who it is as a boy with the 2 girls says Pisces, master as he corrects himself. Your back it's really you right and all 3 of them run down the stairs to Pisces. The 2 girls hug him crying as the boy stands behind them wiping his tears. The girl's say yes yes this is him we would never forget the scent that comes from you when you are playing I mean aura. I move them off me to get a look at them and say who are you 3. One of them looks at me and says you don't remember us. The boy says oh oops we have on our disguise and the other 2 go oh right and take them off. As they do I name them Jesse, Tasha, Jasmine it's you 3. Jesse says yes master when we heard you were back we just had to come to see if it was true. Tasha says you just disappeared after tutoring us in the way of the game we became worried. I said, ``But aren't you guys still at that training camp. As we're talking Lora, and Anne comes to me with worried faces and asks who they are as I'm about to answer Cleo goes ummm aren't we in the middle of something. Tasha walks over to her and says who are you to interrupt us with an intimidating aura. I say no don't but that's when Cleo notices you from the lost element of the storm. Tasha snaps out of it and looks towards Pisces with a worrying look. I say don't I always tell you not to let people know what element you are and tell them to go sit but before you do tell them who you are so we can continue our game. Jesse says I'll go first. I am Pisces first student and am from the fire element.

Then Jasmine goes saying I am his second student and from the element of air. Tasha says I am the final student of his and from the lost element of the storm. I say they are from the training camp I used to go to. We met during my time there when I was there for a year after you guys left. Now go sit down and wait for me. They look at me and say yes sir. I say I know you have questions but let's finish this half and I'll explain with a worried look on Anne and Lora face they say ok. Cleo went to get the ball from the ref to give it to Max to inbound. The game resumes and Cleo gets the ball and goes up the court where she is greeted by Pisces and says so now how would it look if you sat out the 2 quarter with your little pupils here you can't disappoint them now can you master.

CPSIA information can be obtained
at www.ICGtesting.com
Printed in the USA
BVHW041338270122
627375BV00012B/393